P   S

Luna

* * and * *

The Winter

Moon

Festival

Written by G. M. Berrow

ORCHARD

Contents

☆　☆　☆

CHAPTER 1

The Glorious Sun

Darkness covered the spires of the castle and fell over the kingdom. Every corner and curve of the shimmering buildings of Canterlot was covered with the sheen of moonlight. It was a subtle beauty, but a comforting one. Normally, the graceful blue Alicorn felt perfectly at ease during this hour, but tonight was a different story. Tonight she had *social* obligations.

"For Celestia," Princess Luna whispered, reminding herself. She took a deep breath to calm her nerves and peered

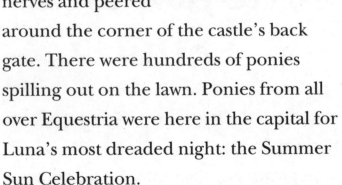

around the corner of the castle's back gate. There were hundreds of ponies spilling out on the lawn. Ponies from all over Equestria were here in the capital for Luna's most dreaded night: the Summer Sun Celebration.

Everypony in Equestria loved the annual event. It was supposed to be a joyous occasion to celebrate Princess Celestia's triumph over the evil

Nightmare Moon. But for Princess Luna it was a reminder of her past mistakes – because she used to be Nightmare Moon, before she transformed back into her true self some moons ago. It was not something she liked to relive.

Luna knew that the Summer Sun Celebration had existed prior to her return. But now she was a leader of Equestria once more, and it was her duty to show her face as the guest of honour. The citizens would expect her to smile and wave, making a rare appearance outside of the ones she sometimes made in their dreams.

A group of palace guards trotted past. Luna could tell they were searching for her. She could delay no longer. It was time. Luna made her way toward the crowd, filled with a sense of dread.

"THOU MAYEST ESCORT ME TO THE CELEBRATION STAGE!" Princess Luna bellowed at the guards. Startled, they whipped their heads toward her, ruffling the blue plumes on their helmets … She cleared her throat, once again surprised by her own voice's volume. Luna lowered her head, and her sparkling blue mane flowed forward. "Excuse me. I kindly beg your pardon, Officers. At large events, I often use the Royal Canterlot Voice. Old habits …" Luna forced a laugh. They smiled back, but she could tell she'd scared them. *Not again*, she thought.

"It's no problem, Princess," said Glimmering Shield, bowing. "Follow me."

Luna nodded to convey her gratitude but didn't speak. She didn't want to make anypony else nervous. The way

Glimmering Shield kept looking back at her over his shoulder as they trotted to the stage made her feel awkward enough. Even after all this time, social skills were something that didn't come as easily to her as they did to Princess Celestia.

As if she could read Luna's mind, Celestia appeared in front of her. "Sister!" she exclaimed, her eyes sparkling with delight. The tall white Alicorn moved toward her, the gold crown atop her head catching the light. "Welcome to the celebration. Everypony is very excited to spend time with you this evening!"

"They are?" Luna asked, scanning the massive crowd. Most of the ponies in sight seemed to be staring at Celestia in admiration. They wore blue, green and purple ribbons in their manes and waved little flags with a picture of the sun on them – just like her sister's famous cutie mark. When their eyes drifted over to Luna, their expressions were a mixture of curious and frightened.

"Of course," Celestia answered. She gestured at the huge crowd with her gold-plated hoof. "Besides, it's one of the only nights when everypony gets to see us together. For some reason, they are still always surprised when you aren't in attendance at the Grand Galloping Gala ..." Celestia laughed, and her almond-shaped eyes crinkled at the corners.

"But I never go!" Luna smiled back. "Why would I change that now?" She always loved hearing Princess Celestia's stories about the Gala each moon, but Luna was very glad that her night shift allowed her to decline attendance. Fancy dresses and small talk were not her idea of a pleasurable evening, though the story from this moon about Discord bringing The Smooze had sounded quite amusing.

The chatter of the crowd gathering nearby in Canterlot's main square was growing louder with each passing minute. They were getting excited. Soon, it would be time for the morning, and Celestia would break the dawn by raising the sun. She would fly up to the sky, spread her wings and use her powerful magic in front of everypony. Until then, Princess Luna couldn't help feeling odd about the fact that the time that normally belonged to her – the peaceful, silent night – was being disrupted. It was just one night.

"Almost time." Princess Celestia nudged Luna. "Are you ready, Sister?"

"WE ARE PREPARED TO PROCEED WITH THE SUMMER SUN CELEBRATION CEREMONY!" Luna thundered.

Celestia giggled and the two sisters stepped on to the stage. They were enthralled by the sight of the joyous citizens of their kingdom and the stars twinkling above.

CHAPTER 2

Royal Business

The three little fillies stared up at Applejack, wide-eyed. They shifted from hoof to hoof anxiously.

"You need to take the train to Canterlot to do what, now?" Applejack, with her yellow mane and brown cowpony hat, said as she made a face that only big sisters were capable of.

"To talk to Princess Celestia about our idea!" Apple Bloom whined. She gave an exhausted sigh and began to pace back and forth in front of her best friends – Scootaloo and Sweetie Belle. Her tiny hooves clip-clopped against the wooden floor of the Sweet Apple Acres farmhouse, and her pink bow bounced up and down. "It's really, really important!"

"Don't go gettin' yer bridle in a twist, now," Applejack said, transferring Golden Delicious apples from a basket to a barrel. The yellow orbs fell into the barrel with a loud series of clunks. "What is it that ya want to tell her? We can write a letter—"

"It's something she'll want to hear about face-to-face, for sure. Official royal business!" squeaked Sweetie Belle. She nodded, her pink-and-purple mane fluffy and her face serious.

"Royal business? Well, why don't y'all talk to Twilight about it?" Applejack shook her head. "She's right down the street, ya know."

"We can't," the three Cutie Mark Crusaders chorused, looking at one another. They were clearly hiding something.

Applejack raised a suspicious brow. "And why not …?"

"Because she already told us to go to Princess Celestia with this particular thing," Apple Bloom lied. "And we can't tell you what it is."

"*Yet*," added Scootaloo. "We can't tell you *yet*."

Applejack saw their expectant little faces and crumbled. Her little sister usually had that effect on her. "All right, all right! Fine. But there is no way I'm lettin' three li'l fillies go to Canterlot all by themselves. Granny'd have my neck faster than ya can shake an apple-seed maraca at a tree bear!"

"We thought you might say that." Apple Bloom smiled, triumphantly. "So we asked Big Mac to chaperone and he said—"

"Eeyup," Big Mac interrupted with a smile, poking his head in through the door. The bulky red stallion stepped inside the farmhouse. He was covered in dirt, but looked pretty pleased about it.

Applejack sighed with a chuckle. "Go on, then, sugarcube. Ya better get washed up and take these youngsters to Canterlot so you can hurry yer hide back here and finish planting the new field."

"Woo-hoo!" squealed Apple Bloom.

"Meet us at the station in ten minutes!" shouted Sweetie Belle as the three friends zipped out the door.

As the Friendship Express chugged through Equestria, Sweetie Belle smooshed her face against the window to get a better look at the passing scenery. Fields of green with splashes of colour zipped by. Sweetie Belle wondered what it looked like at night. Probably pitch-black and scary. It seemed like a good spot for stargazing, though. She made a mental note to consider the spot for a possible party venue.

"Do you think Princess Luna will be mad at us for going behind her back?" Scootaloo wondered aloud to the other two. She could speak freely since Big Mac was definitely not listening. As soon as the train had left the station, he'd fallen asleep. Nopony could hear their conversation over his snores.

"I don't know," replied Apple Bloom. A look of concern flashed across her face. "But maybe. When we saw her in Ponyville last Nightmare Night, she *did* seem a little bit annoyed with us ..."

"I don't know why," Sweetie Belle said, turning to them. "Planning a special festival for Princess Luna is a brilliant idea! There is a Summer Sun Celebration, so why not a winter party for the moon?" The little filly stood up, determination in her eyes. "Besides, we are the Cutie Mark

Crusaders, and it is our duty to help other ponies appreciate their true selves."

"Yeah!" shouted Scootaloo and Apple Bloom together. All three ponies bumped their hooves together.

"Eeyup!" Big Mac added in between snores, causing himself to wake up. He looked around in confusion. The fillies turned to one another and giggled. Even Big Mac agreed and he had been asleep. Now all they had to do was convince Princess Celestia to go along with their plan, too. It would be a piece of mooncake.

CHAPTER 3

An Unwelcome Visitor

The light from the bright moon sparkled on the shifting sea. The sensation of the soft, cool sand on Princess Luna's hooves paired with the sound of silence soothed her after a long night spent watching over Equestria's skies and lands. Guarding the night was no easy task, but somepony had to do it. Princess Luna felt lucky that the job was hers. All those moons spent in exile made her appreciative of everything around her.

Luna settled into a comfortable position, lying down on the sand. She took in the peaceful glow and reflected on the moon. It had gone by so fast! Now that the events of Nightmare Night had passed by, the only thing left was the midwinter holiday – Hearth's Warming Eve. She would never admit it, but it was her favourite one of the whole bunch. There was something undeniably charming about the way white snow shone under moonlight, and the pleasant things ponies dreamed about during the holiday. It was all toys and treats, families and warmth. Togetherness. Luna always looked forward to the holly wreath

Celestia would hoofmake for her and hang on the door of her castle quarters. It was a tradition she'd kept up since they were fillies, when they were just two little Alicorn sisters who had no idea they would someday become the leaders of all Equestria.

No idea that one of them would betray the other some day …

The familiar thought crept into her mind, and Luna tried to gather the strength to push it away. But there she was. Across the water, standing in the ocean, was Luna's worst enemy – Nightmare Moon! The towering dark pony flapped her massive wings and smiled. Her purple armour glistened, wet with sea spray. A devious look shone in her evil, catlike green eyes.

"You can't escape me!" Nightmare Moon cackled, kicking out her front hooves. "I will *always* be a part of you!"

"You may be right about that, Nightmare Moon." Princess Luna stood up, determined. Her flowing mane streamed out behind her as the wind began to pick up. "We shall forever be connected, but your time is finished!" Luna closed her eyes and summoned her magical strength. The wind grew stronger, causing the waves to churn and splash into tall peaks. Nightmare Moon took off.

A blast of light flashed across the ground and spread to the sky. The dreamscape began to crumble and fall apart. In a matter of moments, everything disappeared into a cloud of glittering dust, and Princess Luna sat up. She was in her crescent moon-shaped bed in Canterlot Castle, and it was the middle of the afternoon.

Luna yawned and stretched her hooves out in front of her. She blinked her eyes awake and shook off the sour feeling of the dream.

Thankfully, the appearance of Nightmare Moon in her dreams was becoming more and more rare now that Luna had finished feeling guilty for her actions. Princess Twilight Sparkle and her friends – Pinkie Pie, Rainbow Dash, Fluttershy, Applejack, Rarity, and Spike –

had helped her overcome those emotions. A scary dream creature called Tantabus had threatened both the dream world and Equestria. The more Luna's guilt grew, the stronger the monster had become. It was only when the ponies helped Luna realise that she was punishing herself for her past mistakes that the monster had gone. The sound of distant laughter echoed from the courtyard below, drifting up to Luna's balcony and through the open doors. She left her cosy nest of soft, dark linens and peered down below. There were three little ponies, skipping and giggling.

It was the young ones from Ponyville, accompanied by the big stallion. Luna chuckled to herself, even though she was a little annoyed. Those fillies were persistent, if nothing else.

But it didn't matter. She knew what their plan was and whatever they said, Luna was not going to let them convince her. Her only goal now was to stay out of the spotlight and in the moonlight.

CHAPTER 4

Princess in the Shadows

Princess Luna trotted across the vast quarters, past her star-map-covered walls and the glowing dream orbs that hung from the ceiling. She made her way down the winding staircase, spreading her wings out just enough so that she could float down the steps.

When she arrived at the set of massive arched double doors that led into the throne room of Canterlot Castle, she heard the chatter of voices. The Cutie Mark Crusaders were already inside. They were excited, never letting one another finish a full sentence. She paused for a moment, listening.

But Luna didn't enter the hall. She crept to a side entrance, sneaking through a secret door that led to a balcony overlooking the hall. She flew up and landed softly on the glittering stones. As Luna looked over the balcony, she was careful not to let her midnight-coloured flowing mane give her away.

"And there could be a big ceremony where we drape her in a fancy robe! I'm sure Rarity could sew something really pretty." Sweetie Belle took a deep breath and kept talking. "With lots of stars on it—"

"Games! We could play all of Princess Luna's favorite games!" Scootaloo shouted. "Does she like—"

"Mooncakes?" Apple Bloom asked, hopeful. "Or maybe moon*pies*?"

"These all sound like wonderful suggestions for a Winter Moon Festival." Princess Celestia chuckled. "I'm definitely interested." The three fillies responded with toothy smiles. Princess Celestia stood up and made her way across the room. She paused in front of the stained-glass portrait of her sister. "And you already asked Princess Luna about it?" Celestia asked.

"Well …" Apple Bloom bit her lip.

"We *did* ask her."

"She sorta said no," Scootaloo admitted, looking down at her orange hooves in defeat.

"I'm not surprised …" Princess Celestia furrowed her brow, deep in thought. "But that does present a problem." She motioned for the fillies to come stand beside her. The four of them looked at the picture of Luna as if it would start giving them answers. "My sister is not fond of admiration in the same way she once was."

"Because of when she turned into Nightmare Moon?" asked Sweetie Belle in hushed reverence. Her big green eyes were wide and sparkling.

"That's part of it, Sweetie Belle," Celestia acknowledged. "But it is also another quality in my sister that makes her uneasy around others. It's Luna's nature to seek solace in the places other ponies do not dare go." The Alicorn closed her eyes, unearthing a distant memory. "Did you know that back when we were young princesses, she was the first pony to discover the mountain dragon colonies? And to solve their conflicts with the bat ponies of the western caves?"

"Hot diggity!" exclaimed Apple Bloom. "I did *not*."

Up above, Luna gasped. "My stars …" she whispered, caught off guard by the memory. It had been so thrilling to help the mountain dragons and the bat ponies find peace with one another. Luna always remembered it as one of the first times she'd felt useful as a princess of Equestria, when she'd found her true path to earning her cutie mark.

Scootaloo leaned in. "She did that all *by herself?*"

"That's right." Celestia nodded. A small burst of magical energy emanated from her horn and projected a three-dimensional picture of Luna, standing in between a dragon and a bat pony. It was like a floating snow globe. The Cutie Mark Crusaders cooed.

"At the time, I was so worried that she'd wandered off in the Everfree Forest alone like that." At this, Celestia looked up at her sister and made eye contact. She gave her a little knowing nod.

"But I came to realise over time that Luna will always try to do things her own, special way."

She'd been spotted! Princess Luna recoiled. But rather than revealing Luna's presence to the young fillies, Celestia turned her attention back to the conversation. "Maybe we can find another way to celebrate Princess Luna," she said flatly. "Let's have a look around the castle."

"OK," said the little ponies, slumping in disappointment as they followed the regal Alicorn out of the room. Once they were in the hallway, Princess Celestia made sure the coast was clear of her lurking little sister. Then she bent down, a smile spreading across her face, and whispered, "Or perhaps we could make the Winter Moon Festival a surprise?"

"But what about all that stuff you just said?" Apple Bloom scrunched up her nose in confusion. "About Luna goin' her own way?"

"I just wanted you to understand why she refused your sweet idea," admitted Princess Celestia. "But I think it's finally time for Princess Luna to step into the light again. She is a part of my family and of Equestria."

Celestia used her magic to open a set of doors to a beautiful balcony outside. She conjured up an energy to surround the four of them in a shimmering bubble. Suddenly, a burst of pretty snowflakes began to fall as the light dimmed. A tiny moon rose above their heads, sparkling. The Cutie Mark Crusaders smiled in wonder.

"Besides," Celestia reasoned, and motioned to the life-sized snow globe they were standing in as if it were all the proof she needed, "when is the moon prettier than when it's shining down on the winter snow?"

CHAPTER 5

News from Canterlot

The ride back to Ponyville had felt like an eternity for Scootaloo, Sweetie Belle and Apple Bloom. They were bursting at the seams with excitement since receiving Princess Celestia's blessing. There was going to be a Festival of the Winter Moon to celebrate Princess Luna, and they were going to help plan it! That was, if Twilight Sparkle and her friends agreed to take charge of the event. It was Princess Celestia's one condition.

Once they'd arrived back in town, the fillies didn't waste any time. They trotted straight to the Castle of Friendship to deliver the good news. They pushed through the heavy castle doors, trotted through the cavernous halls and found the throne room. Sure enough, the one dragon and six ponies they were hoping to see were all seated in a circle: Spike, Pinkie Pie, Twilight Sparkle, Rarity, Rainbow Dash, Applejack and Fluttershy. Each was perched upon their respective thrones, identifiable by an image of their cutie mark.

But the little ponies didn't notice that something rather intense was happening.

Rarity and Applejack were speaking in hushed, serious whispers as they consulted the large map of Equestria laid out in the middle chamber. Pinkie Pie furrowed her brow and bit her lip. Fluttershy was on the edge of her seat.

"Whoa," whispered Scootaloo. "Are we about to witness you planning some kind of *secret mission*?"

"Ahem!" Sweetie Belle cleared her throat.

"Girls!" Rarity blushed. "What are you doing here?"

"Yeah!" Applejack added, standing up. "And where's Big Mac? He was s'posed to be watchin' ya in Canterlot!"

"We're back already, and we have big news!" Apple Bloom did an excited jump.

She noticed Twilight and Fluttershy scrambling to gather some little coloured pieces shaped like cupcakes. They were putting them away in a box. "Hey, what's going on here?"

"Uh … nothin'," Applejack stuttered. "I mean *somethin'*, but it's nothin'!"

Pinkie Pie bounced over. "Nothing? It's only the best game EVER, Applejack!"

They were playing a game! "Is it Monopony?" guessed Sweetie Belle.

"No, sillies! We were playing *Whisk*!" Pinkie Pie squealed with delight. "It's the game of Equestrian *domination* where you build bakeries and try to bake more baked goods than other villages can bake, until finally you're the biggest and BEST BAKER IN EQUESTRIA!" Pinkie Pie grinned and held up a hoof-ful of plastic cupcakes. "I was winning."

"That's only because your party cannon artillery took out my cupcake infantry," Rainbow Dash insisted with a shrug. "Lucky roll."

"So what was your big news?" Twilight asked, blushing. She could be so serious that sometimes being seen having frivolous fun caught her off guard. "Did you meet with Princess Celestia? What did she say?"

"Yes!" Scootaloo, Sweetie Belle, and Apple Bloom cheered together.

"She said our idea to hold a Winter Moon Festival in honour of Princess Luna was amazing!" Sweetie Belle squeaked.

"If you need any new outfits for the events, *do* let me know." Rarity nodded.

Then she gave her little sister, Sweetie Belle, a nudge. "You know I can't resist a chance to design something absolutely *gorgeous*!"

"A party?" Pinkie Pie perked up. "I was not expecting that." She narrowed her eyes and looked down at her Party Watch, which bore the word *party* everywhere a number should have been. "Heeeey! This thing must be broken."

"What a lovely idea," Fluttershy remarked. "I'm so glad Princess Luna said it was OK."

Apple Bloom looked at the ceiling. "Well, *she* didn't."

Rainbow Dash and Twilight looked at each other, unsure.

"What Apple Bloom means is, Princess Celestia said it has to be a surprise festival, so we need your help planning it." Scootaloo trotted over to Rainbow Dash and gave her a pleading smile. "Pleeeease?"

"Oh, all right," said Rainbow Dash with a shrug. "It's not like we were busy doing anything important, anyway. Until I have to go up and help with pre-winter cloud arrangement in Cloudsdale, I'm free as a Pegasus."

"Hooray!" the fillies cheered.

Scootaloo shuffled her hoof on the ground nervously. "So … uh, any ideas?"

"Well, it will obviously have to be a classy affair, with elegant and *understated* decorations." Rarity put her hoof to her chin. "What are your feelings on ceremonial capes, hoof-stitched constellation tablecloths, moonflowers around the perimeter of the dance floor, and a hundred-hoof-tall statue of Princess Luna in the centre?" The rest of the group all stared back, faces blank. Rarity clearly had her own definition of "understated."

"What?" Rarity asked. "Too much?"

"No, that sounds awesome," Scootaloo encouraged.

"Yeah!" Apple Bloom agreed. "I like it." She hopped up on to Applejack's throne, which made her feel even more on top of the world than before. "And with all of us working on it together, we're bound to make it just perfect!"

CHAPTER 6

Guardian of the Night

The weeks that followed passed without
event, and Princess Luna thanked her
lucky stars that the Cutie Mark Crusaders'
idea for a celebration had vanished. Luna
was busy enough with winter on its way,
and the last thing she needed to add to
her list was a large event. In addition to

raising the moon and looking after the dream world, the Princess of the Night was a guardian of the creatures of Equestria. Especially the scary, misunderstood ones.

It was a little-known fact that lots of the beasts and creatures were spooked by the idea of winter. Animals ranging from the cragadiles to the cockatrice would sense the impending snowfall and begin to frantically take shelter in caves and burrows throughout the chilly lands. There were always a few scuffles over territory, but over the moons, Luna had become an expert at sorting them out. Most of the time.

This moon the shifting of the seasons had been smooth sailing until tonight. Luna had just returned from her nightly rounds around Canterlot after setting the

moon in the darkened
sky and consulting
her Royal Dream
Register. As
she entered her
quarters, Luna
immediately
noticed a signal on
her special map. It was a
three-dimensional projection, which
appeared like a miniature version of
Equestria spread out across a table. She'd
created it with the help of Star Swirl the
Bearded when Luna was just a young
princess in order to keep ponies and
creatures everywhere safe. It was her way
of seeing the whole kingdom at once.

Princess Luna trotted around to the
other side of the map and bent down.
There was a situation that needed her

attention in the swamplands. A tiny figure of a lion creature with dragon wings appeared next to a beast with the heads of a snake, a tiger and a goat. A disturbance between a manticore and a chimera!

"Castor! Pollux!" Luna called out across the room to two snowy-white owls perched on either side of her bed. "Please watch over Canterlot while I attend to this urgent matter." The owls cooed and flapped their wings in acknowledgement, flying over to their window perches on opposite sides of the tower and setting their yellow eyes on the terrain. Princess Luna nodded her gratitude and trotted over to a cupboard in the corner. She quickly gathered some tools and gave her pet opossum, Tiberius, a little pat on the head. "I shall return soon."

Luna took off into the darkness toward the swampland, her saddlebag full of sweet apples and ricotta cheese. The princess flew through the chilly night air with her beautiful dark wings outspread. And as the wind whipped through her mane, she felt a surge of exhilaration and excitement through her body.

As soon as Luna landed near the site, she spotted the beasts. There were four manticores – a family of two adults and two corelings – growling at the chimera as it circled around the nest they'd hastily built. The creatures all growled and lunged at one another, engaged in an intense standoff.

"Thissss issss our ssspot!" hissed the green snake head of the chimera. "Get lossssst or elssssse!"

"Grrrrrrr!" growled the largest manticore, presumably the father of the clan, as he stood up on his hind paws. He spread his fiery-red dragon wings wide and let out the loudest roar Princess Luna had ever heard! It echoed through the Everfree Forest and beyond. Hopefully it hadn't woken up the entire village of Ponyville.

"IT IS WE, PRINCESS LUNA OF EQUESTRIA, GUARDIAN OF THE NIGHT AND PROTECTOR OF CREATURES

SUCH AS THYSELVES!" Luna bellowed at the group. "WE COMMAND YE TO STAND DOWN!" She shot a blast of incandescent white magic from her horn. The light illuminated the entire swamp and surrounded the beasts. As soon as the magic touched them, all the creatures instantly calmed. They sat down in a haze, blinked their eyes and then turned their heads to face Luna.

"Good." The princess straightened herself and trotted over. "Now, what seems to be the problem, dear citizens?"

After an hour of negotiations, Princess Luna was finally able to resolve the issue with a civilised discussion over a shared feast of sweet apples and ricotta cheese.

Actually it was mainly apples, because the goat head of the chimera ate the majority of the cheese in one bite. But nonetheless, Luna had led them to an agreement.

In the back of her mind, Luna even dared to hope that maybe the creatures would become friends by the end of winter.

"*Friendship*," Luna accidentally said out loud, startling herself. "Oh! That reminds me, I must away. I need to make sure everypony in Ponyville is safe in bed and dreaming soundly …" The princess lowered her front hooves in a deep bow, showing her respect for the chimera and the family of manticores. They bowed back. Then Luna was off, disappearing into the sparkling night.

Chapter 7

Ponyville's Big Secret

A shiver shot down Princess Luna's spine as she landed in the Ponyville town square. And as she exhaled, her breath escaped like a tiny cloud. The Cloudsdale weather factory must be travelling closer – ready to release the first snowfall of the season on this region. It was peculiar, but even Princess Luna still got cold once in a blue moon.

The princess began to walk idly through the streets of Ponyville, listening to her dream senses. If she and the creatures in the swampland had disturbed somepony here, Luna was going to help them. As she turned near Sugarcube Corner, the princess peered up into the windows and listened. But it was just as night should be – lovely and silent. Luna breathed a small sigh of relief and sat down to rest. Maybe it was time to return to her quarters back at Canterlot Castle …

But suddenly something bright caught her eye!

Luna edged closer, alert. But it turned out to be just a pile of party decorations in Pinkie Pie's back garden, glinting in the moonlight. That was nothing out of

the ordinary, reasoned Luna. That pink
pony spent most of her waking hours
entertaining others –
throwing parties, baking
sweets, and making
ponies laugh. Princess
Twilight had informed Luna
that Pinkie Pie had once
thrown eight birthday parties,
two cute-ceañeras, and a foal shower in a
single day.

This was quite the supply of
decorations. Princess Luna trotted over
to the mountain, feeling mildly curious.
They were all in tones of shiny silver,
purple, and dark blue. *Her* colours.
She lifted up a long string of hoofmade
flag bunting for a closer look. The flags
were in the shapes of crescent moons!
Sitting next to them was a giant bag of

uninflated balloons. Luna pulled one out, took a deep breath, and blew into it. Once inflated, it was the colour of midnight and covered in pretty snowflakes and stars. Luna didn't need to unfurl the banner to know what was going on here, but she did anyway.

Winter Moon Festival, it read in huge, glittering letters. *Celebrate Princess Luna!* For a brief moment, her heart softened. Should she let the ponies of Equestria have this one night? Was it her royal duty to let them? But just as a cloud moves swiftly through the dark night, the moment passed. And after it did, Luna knew what just what she had to do.

CHAPTER 8

Dreamwalking in a Winter Wonderland

Tucked up warm in her bed, Apple Bloom was dreaming. "Look, girls!" she shouted. "A shootin' star!" She pointed her hoof at the sky. It was a gorgeous night and the sky was clear and pinpricked with stars.

The field was covered in snow, but the air felt quite warm and comfortable. So strange, this time of moon, but perfect for a party!

"I hope more shooting stars decide to show up once Princess Luna gets here!" added Sweetie Belle cheerily. She was dragging a massive trampoline painted to look like the surface of the moon through the snow. "It really goes with our theme."

"Can somepony help me with these lanterns?" Scootaloo pleaded. She teetered on one hoof at the top of a tall ladder. "I'm too short to reach the string." Her tiny orange wings flapped, but still weren't strong enough to let her fly high enough to reach.

POP!

Princess Luna had entered Apple Bloom's dream in the form of a white bunny with black splotches, mirroring her real-life cutie mark. Since Luna was trying to observe and not to interfere, the little ponies didn't notice her hopping underhoof. She stood up on her hind bunny paws and inspected the scene, nose twitching.

There were tables set up, elaborate game booths, and a dance floor as big as the Canterlot Castle ballroom. A platform stage stood at the front, ready for a big demonstration … like the raising of the moon. It was just as Luna suspected – the three little Cutie Mark Crusaders had gone and planned the Winter Moon Festival anyway!

"I've finished setting up the moon bounce," Sweetie Belle squeaked happily.

"Come on, let's bring out the props for the 'Take a Picture with Princess Luna' photo booth!" The three fillies scrambled toward a big crate and began to pull out hats and fake moustaches. Scootaloo put on a beak and started to dance.

"Squawk!" She giggled, flapping her hooves around. "Look, I'm a chicken!"

A photo booth? Props? How humiliating! This festival had to be stopped, *now*. Princess Luna closed her eyes and readied herself. The trio was so entranced by their own cleverness that they didn't even notice that a few feet behind them, a small bunny was growing to the size of an Alicorn! Magic light surrounding her body, Princess Luna emerged as her regal self.

"Princess Luna!" Apple Bloom spun around, shocked, her pink bow bouncing.

The royal pony bowed her head. "Greetings, young fillies!"

"What are you doin' here?!" Apple Bloom yelped. "The Winter Moon Festival hasn't started yet! It … it's supposed to be a surprise." Her face was filled with disappointment.

"Do you like it?" asked Apple Bloom, motioning to the eyesore around them. "We've been working on this all for you!"

Princess Luna looked around at the set up. There were far too many decorations for her taste. Not to mention that everything was overdone, loud, and exactly as if … a young filly had designed it. Or three of them, to be precise. Apple Bloom, Scootaloo, and Sweetie Belle looked up at her with their large eyes.

"It *is* creative." Luna tilted her head to the side, unsure of how else to react. Even though it was only a dream, Princess Luna didn't want to hurt poor Apple Bloom's feelings. Clearly, the young pony was worried about the event. The fact that she was having this dream proved it.

"Well, phew. That's a relief!" Apple Bloom seemed pleased enough. She looked around with a puzzled expression. "I wonder where everypony is, though. They were supposed to start gettin' here by now." A laugh escaped from Luna as it dawned on her – Apple Bloom still didn't realise that she was dreaming!

Usually when Princess Luna appeared, the dreamer was aware they were being visited in their subconscious. But Apple Bloom was perceiving this exchange as the real event, which meant Princess

Luna could alter it to her liking. She could make this festival as weird and silly as she wanted through the power of dream suggestion. Then Apple Bloom would think it was *her* idea.

If there was one thing Princess Luna couldn't resist, it was a harmless prank. She couldn't help the sneaky smirk on her face as she trotted over to the stage. "Do you mind if I make a few suggestions before the guests arrive?"

"Of course!" The eager Apple Bloom nodded. She scrunched her nose. "Uh … like what?"

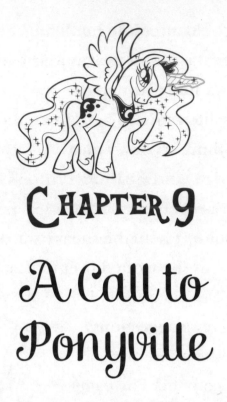

CHAPTER 9

A Call to Ponyville

The next morning, Apple Bloom woke up with the odd feeling that she and the other ponies had been going about this party-planning business all wrong. Instead of decorating with tons of twinkly star lights and moon lanterns, they should make the whole event pitch-black.

So dark that nopony could see anything at all! It was a wild idea, but Apple Bloom couldn't shake it.

The little filly hopped out of bed, ate a quick breakfast of strawberry pancakes with Applejack, and hightailed it over to the Cutie Mark Crusaders' clubhouse for an emergency Winter Moon Festival meeting.

"This meeting of the Cutie Mark Crusaders is called to order!" Apple Bloom announced, banging her gavel on the podium.

"Can we make it fast?" Sweetie Belle yawned. "Something loud woke me up last night."

"Was it a big *rawr* noise?" said Scootaloo. " 'Cause I heard that!"

"No, it was Rarity's snoring." Sweetie Belle chuckled. "You'd never expect it but she really—"

"Come on, girls!" Apple Bloom interrupted. "We *have* to talk about this festival!" Sweetie Belle and Scootaloo exchanged a look as if to say, *What's wrong with her?*

"OK." Apple Bloom unfurled a massive poster and laid it on the ground. A messy hoof-scribbled map of the festival had been drawn on it. She pointed her hoof at the twinkly lights and the lanterns. "We need to get rid of these and these." Then she motioned to the gigantic spotlights that were supposed to shine on Princess Luna as she raised the moon. "And definitely *those.*"

"That's a really strange idea." Scootaloo looked sideways at Apple Bloom. "How are we supposed to see anything without the lights?"

Apple Bloom smiled. "With moonglasses! We need a pair for everypony in Equestria."

When making any official royal visit, Princess Luna traveled by chariot. The two stallions who pulled it were quite unique. Echo and Nocturn were from a race of ponies that lived deep within mountain caves like bats. They had grey hides, pointed wings, yellow catlike eyes and very quiet dispositions.

Luna had found them when she'd responded to a call to go to Smokey Mountain many moons ago, moons after she'd settled the dispute between the bat ponies and the mountain dragons.

The princess had arrived to find the two bat ponies, separated from their colony and caught in the clutches of an angry dragon. Luna had used her Alicorn magic to lull the dragon to sleep, allowing the two stallions to fly away. Deeply grateful for the aid in their escape, Echo and Nocturn had offered to serve as her royal guard.

"Will you be requiring us on your journey to Ponyville today, Highness?" Echo asked with a bow. He squinted his eyes, which were not used to daylight.

"It shall not be necessary," Luna assured him. It had been a long night, but she was excited to see if her little experiment had worked. "I'm only going for a quick surprise visit." She looked to Nocturn, who couldn't even open his eyes. "Besides" – she chuckled – "you two wouldn't be able to see very well in this daylight."

"Not true," Nocturn grunted. He pulled out a pair of shiny sunglasses and put them on. Echo did the same. "We are prepared for all things, Princess."

The princess laughed and took off back toward Ponyville on her own.

CHAPTER 10

The Tarax Hippo

"Princess Luna?" Twilight Sparkle practically galloped over. She moved fast despite the fact that she was carrying a large saddlebag full of books. Her face was the picture of concern. "What are you doing here in Ponyville? Is everything all right back in Canterlot?"

"I assure you that everything is going to be fine, Twilight Sparkle," Luna said.

"Then why are you here?" Twilight's eyes glazed over, searching through the files of her memory, trying to make sense of what the visit might mean. "Is this about the Bugbear? Because he is definitely gone this time. Fluttershy managed to—"

"Twilight!" Luna interrupted. "*No.* It's just a …"

Twilight raised her eyebrows. She was getting suspicious. Luna couldn't tell her the real reason she was in Ponyville.

"A *Tarax Hippo*," Princess Luna improvised, using the name of a creature she hadn't seen in a few hundred moons.

"It's a magical, ghostlike creature that takes up residence in villages just to scare ponies."

"Oh, all right," said Twilight, who appeared relieved at the news. "I thought you might have heard about the fest—" She gasped and covered her mouth with her hoof. "I mean, I'm going to find my friends, and I'm calling a meeting at my castle immediately." She spun around and began to canter away. A few hooves away, she stopped and called out to Luna, "About the Tarax Hippo, I mean! Nothing else!"

"Wait!" Luna shouted. Twilight froze in her tracks and turned around. Luna forced a polite smile. "Thank you, but I insist that there is no need for your interference. As long as I am here, the Tarax Hippo won't come near." Luna wasn't sure if that was entirely accurate, but it didn't really matter. It did the trick.

The Cutie Mark Crusaders' clubhouse sat among the trees in a secluded part of Sweet Apple Acres. Luna hadn't visited the orchard during the day in forever, and she was struck by how beautiful the trees looked. The air smelled chilly and sweet with the scent of apples in the early winter sunshine. Luna's stomach rumbled. She loved apples just as much as anypony else. The princess trotted to the 'free sample' barrel and selected a juicy red one before flying up into a tree outside the clubhouse window.

Inside, the three fillies were opening some giant boxes. "Boy, are we lucky that DJ Pon-3 and Octavia had all these extra moonglasses hanging around in their basement," said Apple Bloom.

"What are moonglasses anyway?" Scootaloo tore open a box and several pairs of glasses went flying across the room. She skipped over and gathered them up.

"They make it so you can see in the dark! You know, like *night-vision*," said Apple Bloom, picking up the pair that had landed by her hooves and popping them on her face. "Also, they make me look really cool." She put her front hooves across her chest. "Deal with it."

Sweetie Belle and Scootaloo giggled.

"OK, the moonglasses I understand, but what's with all the smelly garlic necklaces? Another random idea that just 'came to you'?" Sweetie Belle held up a necklace that was strung with cloves of garlic instead of beads. She stuck out her tongue in disgust.

"Eeyup," Apple Bloom said confidently. "Trust me, I gotta real strong feelin' Princess Luna will like this stuff."

"Yeah, but will anypony else?" Scootaloo murmured to Sweetie Belle.

Princess Luna felt relieved. All she had to do was make a few random suggestions while these ponies were in their dream state, and then this festival Princess Celestia had approved would become absolutely ridiculous. Maybe the whole thing would be so odd that nopony would ever want to have one again! Most ponies already thought Princess Luna was strange. Now the rest of Equestria would, too.

Princess Luna was satisfied. She was about to take off back to Canterlot for some much-needed rest when she heard Sweetie Belle say: "We should probably go and check on Pinkie Pie and Rarity to see how the decorations are coming along."

Apple Bloom nodded. "Then let's stop by Fluttershy's cottage to see how her pet project is going, too."

"Only if we visit Rainbow Dash after that!" Scootaloo called after them. "She was gonna draw plans for those snow castles at the entrance, remember?"

Of course the young ones would ask their mentors for help. Luna put her hoof to her head. She groaned the same way she used to when she and Celestia were fillies and had to do a bunch of chores. Princess Luna was going to have to visit a lot more dreams than she'd anticipated if she was going to sabotage this Winter Moon Festival without hurting anypony's feelings. Why had Celestia agreed to this against her will?

CHAPTER 11

The Royal We

When Princess Luna arrived back to Canterlot, she should have gone straight to bed. But rather than making a rational decision, Luna stormed into the throne room, full of feelings. "HOW COULDEST THOU DO THIS TO US?!" she bellowed, accidentally slipping into her Royal Canterlot Voice.

"Do what, Luna?" A look of concern

flashed across Princess Celestia's face. Luna's eyes had the same crazy expression as they did before she turned into Nightmare Moon! Celestia stood up from her throne and came over to her sister. She put a hoof on Luna's shoulder to calm her. It worked better than a burst of magic. Luna sighed and plopped down on the cold stone floor.

"A Winter Moon Festival?" She hung her head, and her flowing dark mane fell over her green eyes. "What in Star Swirl's bristly beard were you thinking?"

"Oh." Princess Celestia bit her lip. "You found out!" She gave a nonchalant laugh. "It was supposed to be a fun surprise."

"I hate surprises," Luna pouted. "You *know* that."

"But what about all those times in the Castle of the Two Sisters? All those hidden trapdoors and secret passageways you wanted to build into it?" Celestia teased. "I don't recall you disliking surprising Chancellor Puddinghead by jumping out and startling her during royal meetings!"

This memory elicited a tiny giggle from Luna. "That *was* quite amusing …"

"I know." Princess Celestia smiled. "And this will be, too. I promise." Princess Celestia raised her brow in hope. "So will you play along? For the sake of a surprise?"

Luna thought of how determined the little fillies had been in making this happen. If she told Celestia to cancel the whole event now, they'd probably still find a way to surprise her. And then … she'd never know when it was going to be. If Luna went along with the fast-approaching Winter Moon Festival, at least she'd be able to have a hoof in how it went.

"I shall play along," said Luna with a nod. *But there will be some surprises for everypony else,* she thought, imagining the other silly tweaks she could make to the party planners' dreams.

"Thank you, Sister." Celestia bowed. "Now, please go and get some rest. Did anypony ever tell you that you're rather unpleasant when you're tired?"

CHAPTER 12

Dream Team

A strong burst of magic shot from the blue Alicorn's horn and danced its way up to the glowing moon. Luna focused as she gently released the orb from its nightly duty, taking care to lower it, slow and steady. On the opposite balcony, her older sister was focusing hard as well. Celestia was bringing the sun up to hang it in the ever-brightening sky. As soon as the exchange was complete, the two sisters nodded to each other.

"*Gratias lunam et stellas,*" whispered Luna. "Thank you, my dear moon and brilliant stars, for another peaceful night." She trotted inside to take stock of her secret project. Luna flipped open the Dream Register and traced her hoof down the page. It had been a busy week spent visiting almost everypony involved in planning the Winter Moon Festival. Everything was coming together beautifully (or falling apart, like Luna wanted it to). And it was all happening without them even realising it!

In Applejack's dream, Luna suggested that instead of hot apple juice and mooncake as party snacks, they have spicy rainbow juice and banana peel pudding. Another night, Luna influenced

Fluttershy to collect a bunch of hideous blue bugs to release at the party, rather than the cute snow bunnies she planned to have hopping around. And finally, Princess Luna had managed to convince Dream Rarity to sew a bunch of scratchy 'ceremonial cloaks' for the guests to wear instead of pretty dresses. Though, admittedly, that one had taken a lot more work than the others.

Using her magic to close her dark velvet curtains, Princess Luna lay down on her fluffy bed and smiled. She hadn't had this much fun in ages!
It wasn't long until she drifted off into a slumber of her own, dreaming up more silly ways to change the Winter Moon Festival.

"Sorry, Pinkie Pie. I've been so focused on getting these done in time for the Winter Moon Festival." Rarity stifled a yawn. Magic energy flowed out of her Unicorn horn to move a pile of finished ceremonial cloaks. Rarity took another bolt of woollen fabric from the rack and started to roll it out across the cutting table with a sigh. "For some reason, inspiration has struck in the form of cloaks. Would you believe it?!"

"I believe it, and I *like* it!" Pinkie Pie bounced around. She scooped up a robe and tried it on. She began to wiggle and squirm. "Very cloaky ... and so *itchy*! Excellent."

Rarity didn't notice Pinkie Pie doing the itchy dance all around the room. She kept on sewing. "So what were you saying about decorations, darling?"

"Oh yeah," replied Pinkie Pie. "I had this silly, bonkers, wackadoodle-doo idea that we use INVISIBLE decorations instead of the ones with all the moons and stars on them!" Pinkie did a little twirl and singsonged, "So that's what I'm do-o-o-o-oing!"

Rarity gasped and put her hoof to her chest. "*No decorations?*"

"No, silly!" Pinkie Pie giggled. "*Invisible* ones are all the rage these days. I know because I had this amazingly awesome party the other night for Princess Luna and all night she said they were totally her favourite decorations EVER!" Pinkie Pie took off her cloak and bounced to the door. "But I gotta go get to work if I'm ever going to finish them in time for tomorrow. Invisible decorations take twice as much work as regular ones, you know. It's a *quality* issue."

"Whatever you say, darling." Rarity shrugged and adjusted her red glasses. "I'm sure you know what you're doing."

"Of course I do," Pinkie Pie said before she whooshed out the front door. "See ya later, Rarity!"

While it was odd that Pinkie Pie had decided to go minimalist, Rarity wasn't going to press the issue. She had far too much work of her own to do before the Winter Moon Festival. Twelve more pony cloaks and a special one for Princess Luna, too.

In the kitchen, the kettle whistled. "Tea break!" Rarity trotted over and poured herself a steaming cup of rose tea.

She stared out the window of the Carousel Boutique, watching the snowflakes drift down as she sipped her tea. Rarity closed her eyes and floated off into her thoughts, thinking of all the fabulous clothes she'd bought in Manehattan the other day. There was a unique hat she'd just purchased. It was covered in wool and tiny cats and …

"Wait a second! I never bought a hat with cats all over it!" Suddenly, it was like Rarity had woken up from a terrible dream. "That sounds atrocious!"

Rarity jumped up. "And did Pinkie Pie say that she just had a party with Princess Luna" – Rarity narrowed her eyes – "with *no* decorations?"

Something was definitely not right here. Rarity downed her tea in one gulp, fixed her mane in the mirror, and headed straight for Princess Twilight's castle.

Chapter 13

Waking Up

Naturally, the Castle of Friendship was a flurry of activity. Everypony was busy with their individual tasks for the festival. Luckily, Twilight Sparkle had let them use one of the cavernous empty rooms to store all the supplies. Princess Twilight Sparkle's own undertaking – an educational exhibit on the history of the moon phases – was taking up one corner.

There were books, huge display boards and a big model of the moon that ponies could touch.

When Rarity arrived, Fluttershy was leading a parade of ugly blue bugs to a makeshift pen. "That's it, little buggies," Fluttershy cooed. "You're going to spend the night here before Princess Luna's party!" A few of the bugs nuzzled Fluttershy's yellow hoof.

Rarity made a disgusted face. "Fluttershy, dear, what in the world are you doing with all of those things?"

"I got this wonderful idea—" Fluttershy started to say.

"Was it from Princess Luna herself?" Rarity guessed, growing more suspicious.

"Yes, actually," Fluttershy admitted. "She just loves these Ug Bugs so very much. So I thought … why not have them all attend the festival instead of snow bunnies like we planned?"

"Hmmm. Tell me, darling," Rarity asked, raising her hoof and pointing to the hundreds of displaced bugs. "When exactly did Princess Luna tell you that she loves these bugs?"

"It was just the other night, I think." Fluttershy bit her lip, searching. "But we weren't in Ponyville. We were at the Magical Creature Summit and … oh." Fluttershy blushed in embarrassment. "I guess it was just a dream …"

"Aha!" Rarity exclaimed. "Exactly!" She began to pace back and forth. "When I thought of the brilliant idea for cloaks, Princess Luna and I were just arriving back from a day of luxury shopping at Bloomingtail's."

"You went to Manehattan with Princess Luna?" Twilight trotted over, joining in. She cocked her head to the side. "When did you do that?"

"Don't you *see*?" Rarity smiled, triumphant. "I didn't! I just *thought* I did."

"Got the treats!" Applejack trotted into the room, pulling a trolley full of spicy rainbow juice. Behind her, Apple Bloom, Sweetie Belle, and Scootaloo each pulled smaller trolleys filled with banana peel pudding. "So do we!" the fillies chorused.

"Put 'em next to the pile of garlic necklaces in the corner, girls." Then Applejack trotted over to her friends.

"Whoo-ee! I sure am excited that Princess Luna gave me the idea to serve somethin' different to apples this time."

Fluttershy and Twilight's jaws dropped open. Applejack wasn't serving apples? Rarity was right!

"What?" Applejack asked, dumbfounded. "I got a piece o' hay in my teeth or somethin'?"

"No ..." answered Twilight. She trotted over to the mountain of garlic necklaces. "But I think we've *all* got some strange ideas in our heads that were somepony else's."

"What d'ya mean?" asked Apple Bloom, joining in. Beads of nervous sweat began to form on her forehead. "Is this about the garlic? 'Cause we can change that if nopony likes it. I just thought—"

"No, not at all, Apple Bloom." A smile broke out on Rarity's face. "Don't you all see?"

"I see the mess we've made of the Winter Moon Festival," squeaked Sweetie Belle. She hung her head and shuffled her hooves. "What are we gonna do?!"

"Nothing!" Rarity laughed. "Obviously, Princess Luna visited us in our dreams to change the Winter Moon Festival because she knows about the surprise. And *these* are the things she wants at her party! She's just far too shy to tell us."

Chapter 14

Of Great Importance

Since the Summer Sun Celebration was an all-night affair that culminated in hundreds of ponies watching the raising of the sun together at dawn, it was only natural to hold the Winter Moon Festival the opposite way. So it was decreed by Celestia that it would last throughout the day, with the big reveal of raising the moon at dusk. Then the ponies could dance and play beneath the stars until they were too tired to move.

Not that Princess Luna was supposed to know any of this, of course. As far as the ponies in Ponyville were concerned, it was still a big surprise. But today was also the day when all the secret work she'd put into altering the Winter Moon Festival would come to light. Would the ponies realise what she'd done? Would her sister be angry with her for doing so? It was all so unpredictable that Luna actually felt a bit excited about finding out.

It was fortunate that Princess Luna had managed to catch a few hours of sleep after she'd lowered the moon this morning. She wanted to be alert when she made her entrance. Yawning her sleepy

self awake, Luna sipped a
cup of hot chocolate
with whipped cream
and idly trotted
around her quarters,
completing small
tasks from her to-do list.

First, Luna got out her
jewellery polish and shined
each hoofcuff, her crescent moon
neckplate, and her shimmering black
crown. Then she nuzzled Castor and
Pollux, feeling their soft owl feathers on
her cheek as they snoozed away the
morning. After that, she did some leg
stretches with Tiberius.

It wasn't until she was going over her
Dream Register from the previous night
that she noticed something odd. She
pulled out the thread of a dream and

projected it in front of her. As Luna watched, her jaw dropped. Right there, in the dream of a Unicorn named Lyra, was something odd – the Tarax Hippo! The transparent purple Hippo was chasing the mint-green Unicorn through a field, snapping at her as if she were about to become a tasty snack. Lyra howled in fear.

Returning the nightmare to the Dream Register, Princess Luna furrowed her brow in concern. How had it got there? Technically, since the Tarax Hippo had disappeared hundreds of moons ago, there was no way Lyra could even know what one of them looked like. Unless the pony had been studying the creature in a dusty old book! That must have been it, Luna reasoned. Still, it was a strange coincidence, since Luna had used the

Tarax Hippo as her reason for being in Ponyville a few weeks ago.

"Sister!" Princess Celestia exclaimed from just outside the door. "May I enter?"

"You may," Luna replied, hastily closing the Dream Register. Why did she suddenly feel guilty?

Princess Celestia was dressed to impress. The tall, white Alicorn looked ethereal in a gossamer blue gown covered in tiny silver jewels. It draped over one shoulder and gathered around her waist with a string of braided silver rope. And instead of Celestia's usual golden neckplate, her neck bore a delicate necklace made up of glittering stars. She was so stunning, Luna couldn't even speak.

"What do you think?" Celestia lifted up her hoof to show how the beautiful gown sparkled.

"You look beautiful, Sister," said Luna. And she meant it. Suddenly, Princess Luna wished she had something more appropriate to wear. Then her mind drifted to the thought of ceremonial cloaks, and she smirked.

"Here." Celestia produced a shimmering white gown. "I had this made specially just for you. It's the colour of your magnificent moon."

"Wow …" Princess Luna admired the fabric. It was glowing! She was mesmerised. "Thank you," she said gratefully to her sister.

When Celestia departed from the room so Luna could get dressed, Luna felt a mixture of anticipation and nerves in her stomach.

Not long after, the two sisters emerged in the Canterlot Castle square. As Luna and Celestia trotted toward their carriages, the line of guards watched in wonder at the regal siblings.

As Luna trotted past them, each guard bowed deep and said, "*Gratias lunam et stellas.*" That was her special phrase, given each morning to the moon and stars as a thank you. Now it was all directed at her. For once, Princess Luna was surprised! She felt very touched.

"You are of great importance to the ponies in Equestria, Luna." Celestia smiled. "Now do you believe me?"

CHAPTER 15

The Festival of the Winter Moon

"What was I thinking? This has got to be the stinkiest, ugliest festival ever thrown in the history of Equestria!" Rarity cried out, shaking her head in shame. She was wearing her scratchy ceremonial robe.

At least it kept her warm in the snow.

"You got that right!" snarked Rainbow Dash as she flew across the field. She had a clothes peg on her nose to protect her from the stench of her garlic  necklace. "These bat-snowponies Princess Luna asked me to make instead of snow castles look like The Smooze, but with wings." Rainbow patted the side of the batpony she was working on, and the wing fell off. "Make that one wing."

"Not to worry, I can help with that," Rarity said. She shot some magic at the snowponies. It didn't do much good. The thing still looked hideous. "Oh, drat."

"Looooking good!" Pinkie Pie called out. She bounced over. Her fluffy fuchsia mane still managed to bob up and down underneath her cupcake-shaped winter hat. "Hey, they really match the decorations, Rainbow Dash!"

"Pinkie," Rainbow said, touching her hooves down to the snowy ground. "There *are* no decorations, remember? They're 'invisible.'"

"Right ..." Pinkie Pie replied, winking. "You got it."

"OK, everypony, let's all take our places!" Twilight called out from the tent where her educational exhibit was set up. "Princess Luna will be here any moment!"

The townsponies looked at one another in excitement, scrambling to find a good spot to stand when she arrived. The Cutie Mark Crusaders made their way to the front of the crowd. Apple Bloom was a bundle of nerves.

Nopony could see the fear in her eyes while she was wearing moonglasses. "Do ya think she'll like it?"

"She'd better," said Scootaloo with an anxious smile. "Because this stuff is all pretty weird." She gestured to the scene. Ponies were wandering about in brown woollen cloaks, moonglasses and garlic necklaces. There was also the horde of Ug Bugs, and an educational tent. There were no pretty lights or decorations anywhere.

"I know." Sweetie Belle bit her lip. "Plus, that banana-peel pudding is the yuckiest thing I've ever tasted."

"You two aren't helpin' me feel better, ya know," griped Apple Bloom, frowning. She straightened up. There was one thing left that she had to be proud of. "At least I invited some special guests."

"Who are they?" Sweetie Belle asked.

"It's a surprise!" Apple Bloom reminded her with a smile. "Stop askin' me! You'll see."

The hubbub of the crowd grew louder, and Apple Bloom looked at the sky. The princesses of Equestria were approaching in their carriages! In the front was Princess Celestia, her sparkling white carriage pulled by two royal guards of the sun. Behind her was the guest of honour herself, Princess Luna. Her two bat-pony guards, Echo and Nocturn, soared toward the field.

"There they are!" the ponies called out in excitement.

The princesses landed softly on a bank of snow and trotted over to the

festival entrance. Twilight Sparkle and all her friends cantered over and lined up to greet them.

"Hide me!" cried Rarity, looking down at her cloak. "Now Luna's here this all seems like a big mistake! It all seemed better in theory!"

"'Welcome, Princess Luna!'" Apple Bloom read from a scroll. "'In-honour-of-all-that-you-do-and-the-moon-up-above, we-have-planned-this-here-First-Annual-Winter-Moon-Festival!'" Apple Bloom forced a big, cheesy smile. "'A-new-royally-decreed-holiday!'"

"Surprise!" the ponies cheered. "Yay, Princess Luna!"

Luna stood, frozen. Her face was blank. She momentarily forgot that she was supposed to be acting surprised! Princess Celestia gave her a little nudge, as if to say, *Remember our deal?*

"My stars!" Princess Luna gasped. "Thou didst this all ... for me?" She motioned to the snowy field full of bugs and garlic. She bowed, stifling a giggle. "Thank you, dearest ponies of Ponyville. It's wonderful." Princess Luna trotted toward the crowd. She took in the silly scene, admiring how flawlessly the ponies had executed her odd suggestions. Every single weird and wonderful thing she'd asked for was there.

"Wow," Luna whispered to herself, finally understanding what her sister had been trying to tell her. This was different from the Summer Sun Celebration or Nightmare Night. This wasn't a holiday dedicated to her mistakes as Nightmare

Moon. This was a party meant to celebrate everything she'd done right. And she'd ruined it!

Suddenly, a series of loud screams came from the back of the crowd.

Chapter 16

A Lively Affair

"STAND BACK!" Princess Luna barrelled through the crowd. The screams were coming from a mint-green Unicorn who was wearing a garlic necklace. Luna recognised her immediately – it was the same pony that she'd seen in the dream earlier, Lyra!

"What happened?" Princess Luna was on high alert, searching the horizon. "What hath terrified you so?"

Lyra was shaking. "It was a … a … a beast!" They weren't too far from the Everfree Forest. It could have been anything. "A ghost-beast!"

"Over there!" shouted a purple Pegasus. "It's coming back!"

Luna couldn't believe her eyes. It was actually a *Tarax Hippo*!

The massive grey ghost was running right towards the party! The monster looked almost the same as a normal hippopotamus, except with pointy teeth, and a shimmering, translucent body. And his prime objective was to terrify ponies. Princess Luna would not have that. "Everypony in that tent!" She motioned to Twilight to guard the townsponies.

Princess Celestia soared over and took her place next to her sister, ready for a fight. The Alicorns pushed their hooves into the snow, standing solid. Celestia looked to Luna. "I have not seen a Tarax Hippo in hundreds of moons. Why is he here?"

"I think it might be my fault!" Luna called out, remembering her little white lie to Princess Twilight weeks ago. "I must have accidentally summoned him!"

The Tarax Hippo ran toward them, letting out a low, guttural noise. Sounds of shrieks escaped from the tent. The Tarax Hippo smiled, then began to grow.

Celestia fired a zap of pink energy at the beast to contain him. But the magic shot straight through and hit a nearby tree, melting the snow on its branches. "Luna! How do we calm him?"

The Tarax Hippo set his sights on the tent full of ponies. The tent rustled around, packed to capacity. The Tarax Hippo paused to smell the air before moving toward it.

"What does he want?" Luna whispered to herself, flying around to head him off. Then she saw it. A sack full of garlic necklaces. Luna called out to her sister, "It's the garlic!"

"You are right, dear Luna of the night!" Zecora the zebra called out as she emerged from the Forest. "Throw the garlic! You must! It's the only way to gain his trust!" Zecora advised.

Princess Luna swooped down, snatched the bag of necklaces, and tossed them at the Tarax Hippo. He opened his slimy mouth wide and caught them in one gulp. He chomped down in satisfaction. As he chewed, he became smaller. Luna smiled triumphantly. "Citizens! Throw your garlic necklaces at the beast!"

"But be gentle, everypony," Fluttershy told them. "He's just a creature that's lost his way."

Twilight Sparkle, Rainbow Dash, Rarity, Fluttershy, Pinkie Pie, and Applejack ran toward the Tarax Hippo. They created a circle around him, herding him just like Applejack did with the sheep back at Sweet Apple Acres.

"We're not afraid of you!" shouted Rainbow Dash, tossing a garlic necklace. He caught it in his mouth and licked his lips. "Except maybe your breath later!"

"Wow!" Pinkie Pie squealed. She ran out of garlic, so she began to toss random items such  as snowballs and bowls of banana-peel pudding. "He's hungry! Like … *hungry, hungry!*"

"Princess Luna," Twilight called out, "what next?"

Before Luna could answer the question, one of the manticores from the swamp swooped down and landed in front of the Tarax Hippo. "RAAAAAAAWR!" he roared. The Tarax Hippo immediately fell into a trancelike state. Then he sat

down with a big *thud* and fell asleep.
Princess Celestia flew over. She bent
down, used her magic to surround the
Tarax Hippo, and gently whispered a
spell. The beast floated off into the
Everfree Forest, back to his sleepy cave.

It was over.

The ponies applauded, surrounding
Princess Luna.

The bat ponies, the mountain dragons
and the manticore joined in.
They bowed to Luna and turned to the
ponies. "Y'all came!" Apple Bloom
jumped up and down with glee. "I invited
'em and they came!"

Zecora stepped forward and started
talking in rhyme, as always. "Thanks to
Luna, we've settled our score, and these
noble creatures are no longer at war," she
explained. "Though it was many moons

ago, thanks to her, peace we owe."

One of Luna's guards, Nocturn, stepped forward. He bowed his head to Princess Luna and turned to the crowd. "And for this, tonight we celebrate our dear Princess of the Night – Luna the Great!" Everypony cheered and gathered around to hear more stories of Princess Luna's trials. Looking at the happy faces all around her, Princess Luna had never felt so loved.

Chapter 17

Luna in the Light

After the exciting battle with the Tarax Hippo, the ponies were in the mood to party – even Princess Luna. While the festival was strange, it fit Luna just right. She was different to her sister, and she always had been. This celebration was proof of that.

Princess Luna laughed with the townsponies, who were dressed in their funny ceremonial clothing. They had put this all together, just to make her feel special. Even the manticore stuck around, making new friends and tasting the spicy rainbow juice. It made Luna feel warm and fuzzy, even in the snow.

"It's extraordinary, isn't it, Sister?" Celestia said, watching the peculiar party. "That we have the privilege of protecting and knowing such wonderful citizens?"

"Yes," Luna admitted. "You were right. Thank you for allowing the festival, even when I did not." She nodded to her sister and held out her hoof. Celestia shook it.

"Strange choice of theme, though," Celestia marvelled. She pointed to Rarity, who had turned her itchy cloak into a surprisingly nice one-shouldered gown.

"I'm surprised they let the little ones choose all these odd details!" She laughed. "What are these strange outfits? Why are there bugs everywhere?"

"Well, I may have had something to do with that ..." Princess Luna admitted with a giggle. "I suggested some things while the ponies were dreaming. It turns out it works quite well!"

"Luna!" Celestia's eyes grew wide in shock. "You didn't!"

Luna smiled. "But I think it's time for the real celebration to begin!"

Luna focused her magic. The whole field began to transform into the winter wonderland the ponies had imagined. Soon, there were glittering snow castles and twinkling lights everywhere. Chocolate fountains and bubbling pots of hot apple juice hovered next to trays upon trays of mooncakes and apple turnovers. The Ug Bugs floated up into the air, spreading their wings and glowing. They danced around like stars in the darkening sky.

"These invisible decorations are really starting to come alive," Pinkie Pie joked. "This is beautiful!" Twilight said.

It was the true Winter Moon Festival, just as it was meant to be.

"I'm sorry that I altered your plans, dear friends," Princess Luna said solemnly. "I was hoping to ruin the party because I did not feel worthy of one." She turned to the Cutie Mark Crusaders and smiled. "I know now that that is not true. It is such a gift to know that you have ponies that care for you so much, as you all do for me." She motioned to their surroundings. "So as my gift back to you, here is *your* festival!"

The ponies surrounded Luna and gave her the biggest group hug. Princess Luna felt so on top of the world, she could raise a thousand more moons.

Read on for a peek of Princess
Celestia's exciting
My Little Pony adventure,

Princess Celestia and the Royal Rescue

The sunlight dappled across the castle floor in multicoloured shards, softening the appearance of the chequered stones. The gentle haze of daybreak had always been Princess Celestia's favourite time. Not just because she was in charge of raising the sun. To her, the dawn was a peaceful and quiet promise of things to come – the activities of an exciting day still lay ahead of all the ponies in the land. Today would be a beautiful sunrise.

Celestia turned to the sun and focused

her magic. She watched the progression of the golden orb climbing higher into the sky, turning her attention back to the pattern projected on to the floor with the focused care of an artist creating a grand masterpiece.

Even though this picture was one that the princess had painted the same way each morning for hundreds of moons, she gave it the same care every single day. It was her honour and her duty.

The pieces of stained glass set in the centre of the main arched window depicted Equestria's newest princess – an exceptionally talented young scholar named Princess Twilight Sparkle. The new royal and her five best pony friends and dragon assistant, whose images were immortalised in the glass as well, had protected Equestria from peril on more than one occasion. They now nobly sought to spread the true spirit of the Elements of Harmony and, in turn, the Magic of Friendship across its lands.

Twilight Sparkle, Rainbow Dash, Rarity, Pinkie Pie, Applejack, Fluttershy and Spike had come a long way since they'd all become friends. Celestia beamed with pride whenever the young heroes graced her thoughts or when their image in the window caught her eye.

A prominent piece of purple glass in the window cast a glow in the shape of a star on the centre tile of the floor, signalling that the morning process was almost complete. Celestia closed her almond-shaped eyes, and her dark lashes pressed down in stark contrast against her white cheekbones. She mustered every inch of strength in her body. She felt herself glistening with magical energy, from the bottom of her gilded hooves to the edges of her flowing mane of lavender, pale green and periwinkle blue, and bursting out to the very tip of her long, pearled horn. When Celestia opened her eyes again, the sun had reached the highest peak of its arc in the sky. The world was bright.

"*Gratias ad solis ortum,*" the princess recited as she bowed deeply to the sun. "Thank you for allowing me to guide you, and thank you for another day of light."

"Beautifully done, sister."

"Thank you, Luna." Celestia smiled without turning around. "I did think that sunrise was particularly smooth."

"'Twas, indeed." Princess Luna stifled a yawn as she stepped forward to meet her elder sister. The contrast of the rich, velvety darkness of Luna's blue coat next to Celestia's pale, pearly complexion was stark. It mirrored the colours of the skies that they each watched over. Light and dark. Night and day.

But the sisters were not so different. In addition to raising the sun and the moon, they both ruled over Equestria, protecting its inhabitants from harm.

"You seem more exhausted than usual, Luna." Celestia furrowed her brow in concern as her sister yawned again. "Was the night not tranquil?"

"I must confess," Luna offered with a deep exhalation, "I am feeling the effects of a night-time most threatened." She pointed her hoof toward the eastern window of the throne room. "There is peril on the coast."

"The coast? Tell me, sister," Celestia urged. "What happened? Is there anything I need to attend to on this day?" Celestia tried to remain calm as she spoke her words. Perhaps it was because she'd had hundreds of moons of experience dealing with crises under her crown, or perhaps she knew that panicking was the quickest way to derail a solution. Deep breaths and a steady voice were the key. Always maintain a calm composure, and those around would follow suit.

Princess Luna shook her head. Her dark, flowing mane billowed around the sides of her face. "It was a manticore disturbance on the coastline," she explained, lifting her hoof toward the east. "I was able to reason with them. Until the Carcinus showed up … *He* came out of nowhere." She raised her brow in mild exasperation. Luna was tough, so this signalled to her sister that the disaster was worse than she was saying.

Celestia stiffened. "Carcinus again?" she said with a frown, picturing the beast in her mind. The giant crab species were the size of small buildings and could be quite temperamental. But they were also gentle and understanding. A pony just had to know how to talk to them, to use kindness. "There have been far too many disturbances for my liking as of late. Perhaps I should not go to Monacolt after all. I'll just head to Horseshoe Bay and—"

"Sister, *no*." Luna stepped in to block Celestia's path to the door. Her face grew stern. "You must keep your promise to Duchess Diamond Waves. You're the only pony who can help her, correct?"

"She seems to believe that the students at her magic school need my help." Celestia bit her lip and reconsidered.

It was a struggle for her to relinquish responsibility of Equestria by leaving the capital, but even more of a struggle to let down an old friend in her hour of need. Finally Celestia nodded. "You're right. I must go to her. With any luck, I'll have the students of Monacolt back on track within a few risings of the sun."

Celestia glided toward the balcony again, and Luna soon stood beside her. Both princesses watched over the stirrings of the waking city below in silent reverence. The Canterlot ponies were just beginning to fill the cobblestone paths.

A pair of royal guards in their golden armour trotted toward the castle, their blue-feathered helmet plumes bobbing up and down as they stepped in time. Across the main plaza, a milk pony was making his morning rounds and placing glass bottles of fresh cream in front of each café and residence. On the other side, a group of rambunctious colts and fillies trotted together, giggling and teasing one another. Celestia smiled to herself as she watched them surreptitiously. Her young unicorn students were vivacious – bright as the sun and bursting with talent. *What could be so different about the students at Diamond Waves's academy?* Celestia wondered. Whatever the reason for their struggle, Princess Celestia was about to find out. She'd be lying if she said she wasn't intrigued by the adventure.

"You're positive you can handle Canterlot on your own?"

Princess Luna raised an eyebrow at Celestia. "Are you really asking me that again?" The blue mare trotted around her sister in a circle, wondering if her sibling would ever learn to trust her. Celestia hardly ever let anypony know when she was worried, but Luna could always tell. And right now, Celestia's golden neckplate jewellery was on slightly crooked. Otherwise, Celestia was the picture of perfection.

"I know I need to start my journey, for it is long, but I just want to be absolutely sure," Celestia replied from the seat of the carriage. A soft pink glow came from her horn. She lifted a saddlebag bearing a picture of her golden-sun cutie mark on to the seat next to her. "Even with the situation at Horseshoe Bay?"

Luna sighed. "I wish you would have more faith in me, Celie."

"I do, it's just that—"

Luna's face grew serious. "All right,

you caught me. I'm planning to transform to Nightmare Moon mode as soon as you leave the border!" It was her favourite way to tease Celestia. After Luna had acted up and been banished to the moon, her sister was very touchy about the subject. But the two sisters were past that now. Celestia rolled her eyes, and Luna's face broke into a devious smirk. "Just messing with you, sister. I know that you worry about me watching over the day, so I've brought in somepony who is very competent to help out at your school and to look over Canterlot while I rest."

"Surprise!" A purple Alicorn with a pink star-shaped cutie mark trotted up to meet them. "Princess Luna said you needed a little bit of assistance."

"Twilight Sparkle!" Celestia exclaimed, embracing the pony. "What a pleasure it is to see you again, my faithful student. I hope you're not too put out by this request."

"Not at all, Princess," Twilight replied with a grin. "I can think of nothing more exhilarating than watching over your class for a few days." Twilight revealed a gigantic cart full of books. "In fact, I've even brought some special reading material that I know your students will be delighted with! I can't wait to discuss Wing Theory with them. Have you guys covered metamorphosis spells yet? Maybe I'll start with the good old apple-to-orange experiment." Twilight laughed and added, "I'll make sure all the class frogs are out of the room for that one." She winked. Twilight had once accidentally transformed a poor frog into an orange by mistake.

"Thank you." Celestia smiled.

"Whatever lessons you decide to work on, I know my colts and fillies are in good hooves. But, Twilight?"

"Yes, Princess?" Twilight perked up, eyes wide and purple wings outspread.

"Please make sure they have a little *fun* as well, OK? It's almost the summer break, for Star Swirl's sake." Celestia nudged the young Alicorn with her hoof. "You have a good time, too."

Luna giggled. Twilight crinkled her eyes in confusion. "What's not fun about speed-reading the entire *Encyclopedia Equestria?*"

Celestia laughed, patting her faithful student on her purple mane. "You let me know when you figure it out, Twilight."

"Oooh! With a letter update?" Twilight Sparkle brightened. "Just like I used to?"

Celestia's thoughts flashed to the

mountain of letters from Twilight that filled one cupboard of her bedroom quarters. "On second thoughts, only send me a letter *if necessary* – to update me on the kingdom news. You and Princess Luna together, OK?" That seemed to be a good compromise and a perfect way to set Celestia's mind at ease.

Read
Princess Celestia and the
Royal Rescue
to find out what happens next!

Turn the page for a
special surprise from
Princess Luna!

Dearest reader,

I created these bonus pages

by the light of the moon

just for you! Enjoy the activities and

don't forget to share them with your

friends.

Yours in nighttime,

Princess Luna

Dream Journal

From time to time, Princess Luna visits ponies in their dreams. She tries to help them realise their true feelings about the events happening in their lives. Have you ever had an interesting dream that you wanted to remember? Use these pages to record your dreams!

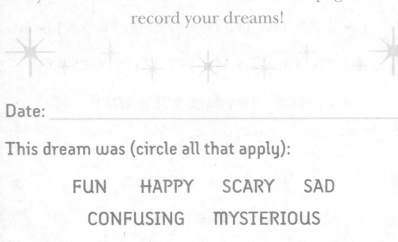

Date: _____

This dream was (circle all that apply):

FUN   HAPPY   SCARY   SAD

CONFUSING   MYSTERIOUS

Dream description: _____

_____

_____

_____

_____

_____

Date: _____

This dream was (circle all that apply):

FUN   HAPPY   SCARY   SAD

CONFUSING   MYSTERIOUS

Dream description: _____

_____

_____

_____

_____

_____

_____

_____

_____

_____

_____

_____

_____

Date: _____

This dream was (circle all that apply):

FUN   HAPPY   SCARY   SAD
CONFUSING   MYSTERIOUS

Dream description: _____

_____

_____

_____

_____

_____

_____

_____

_____

_____

_____

_____

Map to the Stars

As guardian of the night, it is Princess Luna's job to look after all of Equestria once the sun goes down. She makes sure the ponies are safe and the stars and moon are glittering in the sky. Tonight, the clouds are hanging low, covering her favourite constellation. Can you help Luna see the picture by connecting the stars?

Snowpony Couture

The Cutie Mark Crusaders have built some snowponies for the Festival of the Winter Moon! Can you help the trio decorate this one? You can make it look pretty or silly – anything you think Princess Luna might like!

Sister Surprises

Princess Celestia loves her little sister, Luna,
so much that she agrees to help the
Cutie Mark Crusaders plan a big surprise.
Have you ever planned a big surprise for someone
in your family? If so, what was it? If not, what would
you do for a family member if you could?
Write about it here.

_____

_____

_____

_____

_____

_____

_____

_____

_____

Pony Pyjama Party

The ponies are planning a slumber party so they
can stay up all night and stargaze! Take turns
with a friend connecting the stars to make the
boxes. Write your initials in each completed box
for one point. The player with the
most points (and boxes) wins!

MARE IN THE MAZE

Princess Luna is having a terrible nightmare that she is Nightmare Moon again! Can you help her find her way out of the maze and back to her true pony form

START

FINISH

Winter Warm-Up

Even Princess Luna gets chilly in the winter! Help her get dressed for the Festival of the Winter Moon by designing her outfit. Be sure to make it stylish and cosy! (Hint: Luna's favourite shapes are crescents and stars.)

A Bountiful Buffet

The Cutie Mark Crusaders are working hard to get the refreshments ready for the festival! So far, they've baked a bunch of moonpies and collected some barrels of juice. What other kinds of snacks should they have at the festival? Circle or colour all the treats that you think might be perfect!

Searching for Luna

The ponies in Canterlot are looking for Princess Luna so she can raise the moon, but she is nowhere to be found! Has Luna disappeared again? Find the words in the search to help bring Luna back to the castle.

```
S  U  R  P  R  I  S  E  N  L
T  J  N  E  N  L  B  I  G  A
A  L  A  W  U  I  G  S  Q  V
R  K  C  N  O  H  G  F  J  I
S  U  A  M  T  N  L  H  V  T
N  O  O  M  F  F  S  N  T  S
R  J  A  O  G  S  Y  E  R  E
E  R  O  C  I  T  N  A  M  F
E  U  B  D  A  F  N  S  W  L
Y  N  L  S  H  E  K  G  T  W
```

FESTIVAL   MOON   SNOW

LUNA   NIGHT   STARS

MANTICORE   NIGHTMARE   SURPRISE

Look out for the new series from the creators of My Little Pony

Join Blythe Baxter and her friends at the Littlest Pet Shop – a world of pet pals, fashion and fun!

Feb 2016

Feb 2016

Apr 2016